In the year 2065, secur...
teed for everyone on Earth by ...
Security Patrol. Led by the resourceful Commander
Shore, W.A.S.P. exists to combat threats to world
peace.

Threats such as that posed by Titan, tyrant of the
ocean bed, overlord of the inhuman Aquaphibians. He
has sworn to destroy W.A.S.P.'s base at Marineville,
leaving himself undisputed master of the seas.

Pride of W.A.S.P.'s futuristic fleet is Stingray, the
state-of-the-art submarine. Stingray is captained by
Troy Tempest who, along with his loyal first officer,
Phones, is always on the alert to foil evil under the
sea. And they are aided in this mission by Marina,
maiden of a strange undersea race, who was Titan's
slave before rescue by Troy and Phones.

Back at base, they can always count on support
from Atlanta, the commander's strong-willed
daughter, and other stalwarts such as Lieutenant
Fischer, who mans Marineville's control tower.

Together, they form W.A.S.P.

# STINGRAY

## THE DISAPPEARING SHIPS

WASP

## Dave Morris

3

YOUNG CORGI

STINGRAY: THE DISAPPEARING SHIPS
A YOUNG CORGI BOOK 0 552 52780 7

First publication in Great Britain

PRINTING HISTORY
Young Corgi edition published 1992

Set in 14/18pt Linotype New Century Schoolbook by
Phoenix Typesetting, Burley-in-Wharfedale, West
Yorkshire.

Young Corgi Books are published by Transworld
Publishers Ltd, 61-63 Uxbridge Road, Ealing,
London W5 5SA, in Australia by Transworld
Publishers (Australia) Pty. Ltd, 15-23 Helles
Avenue, Moorebank, NSW 2170, and in New
Zealand by Transworld Publishers (N.Z.) Ltd,
3 William Pickering Drive, Albany, Auckland.

Made and printed in Great Britain by
Cox & Wyman Ltd, Reading, Berks.

# THE DISAPPEARING
# SHIPS

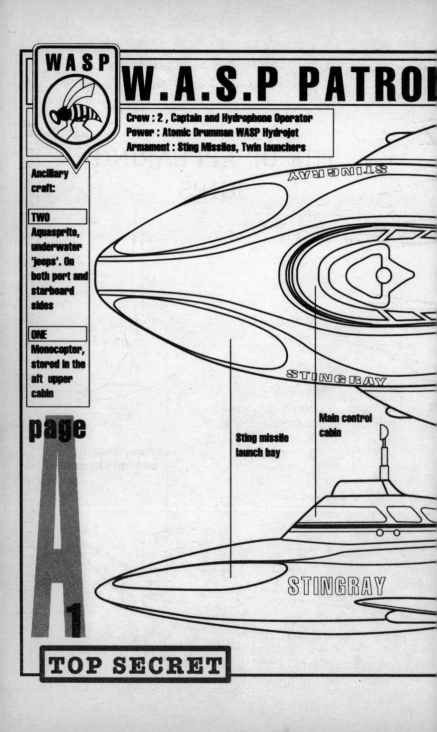

# WASP

# W.A.S.P PATROL

Crew : 2 , Captain and Hydrophone Operator
Power : Atomic Drumman WASP Hydrojet
Armament : Sting Missiles, Twin launchers

**Ancillary craft:**

**TWO**
Aquasprite, underwater 'jeeps'. On both port and starboard sides

**ONE**
Monocopter, stored in the aft upper cabin

page
A
1

STINGRAY

STINGRAY

Main control cabin

Sting missile launch bay

STINGRAY

TOP SECRET

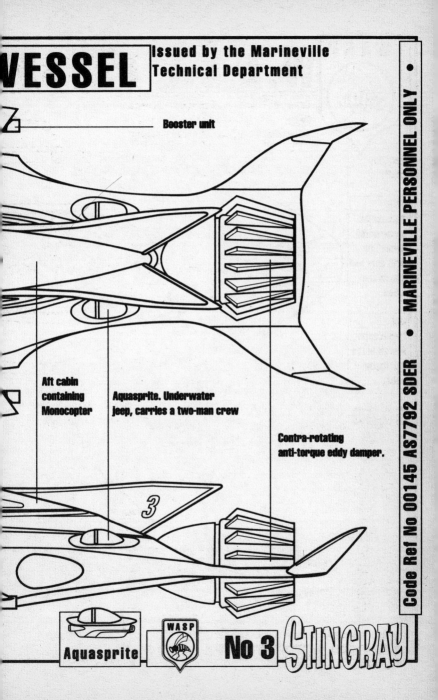

# VESSEL

Booster unit

Aft cabin containing Monocopter

Aquasprite. Underwater jeep, carries a two-man crew

Contra-rotating anti-torque eddy damper.

3

Aquasprite

WASP

No 3 STINGRAY

MARINEVILLE PERSONNEL ONLY • Code Ref No 00145 AS7792 SDER

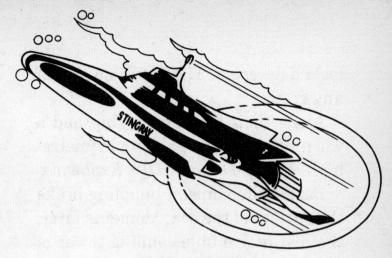

## *Chapter One*
## WASTE DISPOSAL

Under a sky that was just turning the colour of autumn leaves, three huge freighters sailed slowly eastwards. They were of an old design, nowadays obsolete, and rust had spread in patches across their hulls. They didn't look in any shape to be carrying cargo across the ocean. A closer look would have revealed an even stranger thing – all three ships looked deserted. There was no sign of any crew.

Along their bows, each ship had a warning message painted in metre-high letters: *Danger High Explosive*.

Beside the ships, a bubbling broke the surface of the sea. Moments later, the distinctive blue conning-tower of Stingray rose through the waves.

Troy set Stingray on automatic to cruise alongside the three freighters. 'OK, Phones,' he said, 'time to go aboard.'

The two men went out on to Stingray's prow and climbed the rungs up to the deck of the first freighter. Here on the bridge, where you might have expected to find the ship's wheel, was a bank of computer equipment. It was steering the three ships automatically.

Troy went over and punched in

an access code. Then he released a safety lock which opened a small panel in the base of the computer console. There were three switches there, and he set them all in the on position before replacing the panel.

*Detonation sequence active*, read a message on the VDU. *Detonation to commence in* 09:59 *hours*. As they watched, the VDU display began its relentless countdown.

'Well, that's that,' declared Troy. 'These old hulks will be nothing but scrap metal by tomorrow morning.'

Phones nodded. 'I'd better check the automatic bos'un. We want to be sure they're heading for the right part of the ocean.'

Phones keyed in a few commands and checked the read-out against a map. 'Yeah,' he said, 'everything's ship-shape. They'll explode right over the mid-Atlantic trench. Any debris that's left after the explosion will just sink down and be lost for ever.'

'Excellent,' said Troy. 'It's pollution-free waste disposal. Amazing, isn't it, Phones? Not that many years ago, valuable man-hours would have been wasted dismantling obsolete old hulks like these.'

'And there'd have been the problem of left-over rust and nuclear waste afterwards,' added Phones. 'Now it's simple: we just send them out to the middle of the ocean and blow them sky high!'

Troy checked his watch. 'We ought to be getting back to Marineville,' he said.

'Say, that's right,' agreed Phones. 'We're supposed to be going round to the commander's place this evening. It wouldn't do to keep him waiting.'

With a last glance around the silent ships, they returned to Stingray. Troy flooded the ballast tanks and Stingray submerged. Waves surged up past the viewports – green murky water replacing the faintly melancholy sight of three great ships heading silently out to sea in the red glare of sunset.

'Atlanta!' thundered Commander Shore. 'We're waiting for you.'

From Atlanta's room there came the sound of drawers and cupboards being turned out. They heard her give an exasperated growl. 'You'll just have to go ahead without me, father,' she called back. 'I'm busy.'

Commander Shore sighed. 'She says she's busy . . .'

'She certainly sounds it,' said Troy with a smile. 'Let's start, then.' He dealt a hand of cards to each of them,

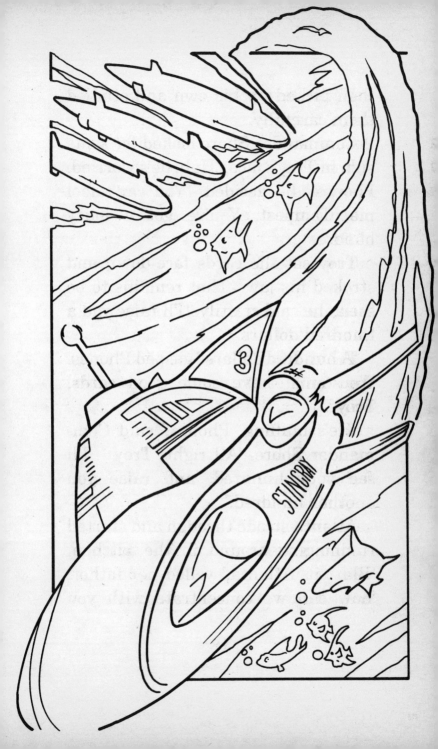

then picked up his own and studied them carefully.

Commander Shore looked for some sign in Troy's face. 'Hah, he's worried, Phones!' he decided. 'You can't fool me, Tempest. You've got a lousy hand.'

Troy set the cards face-down and stroked his jaw. 'That remains to be seen,' he said craftily. 'I'll raise you a hundred dollars.'

'A hundred dollars!' gasped Phones. 'You must have some good cards, Troy.'

'He's bluffing, Phones,' said Commander Shore. 'All right, Troy – I'll see your hundred, and raise you another hundred.'

Atlanta strode through and started rummaging around in the kitchen. 'Blast it, Atlanta,' yelled her father, 'how can we concentrate with you making such a racket? What are you looking for, anyway?'

'It's an old chocolate box,' replied Atlanta. 'Have you seen it, father?'

'Chocolates?' said Commander Shore. 'Nasty sweet things! I never touch them.' He turned back to the card table. 'Well, Troy, are you going to call, or stack?'

Troy showed his cards to Marina, who was not playing but was sitting on the arm of his chair and giving him advice. She nodded. 'All right,' he said, 'I'll raise you *one thousand* dollars, and I'll see you.'

'One thousand!' exclaimed Phones. 'This game's too hot for me . . .'

Troy laid out his cards, two jacks and two kings. But Commander Shore had a better hand. He beamed in triumph as he showed them: three aces and two eights. Full house.

Commander Shore couldn't help chuckling as he tallied the score to date. 'Hmmm . . . that makes seven million, three hundred thousand and eighty bucks you now owe me, Troy.'

Troy gave a rueful smile. 'I guess I'm just not lucky,' he said.

Atlanta emerged from the kitchen and stood in the doorway, hands on hips, looking around for some corner of the apartment she had not yet

searched. 'Are you *sure* you haven't
seen that box?' she asked her father.
'It had a picture of a kitten on the
lid.'

'Oh, *that*,' said Commander Shore.
'Yeah, I put it in the waste disposal.
For crying out loud, Atlanta, it was
just an empty box.'

'I might have found a use for it!'
fumed Atlanta.

Commander Shore shook his head.
'If one of us didn't throw things out
now and again, Atlanta, this whole
apartment would be stacked to the
ceiling with junk.'

'Atlanta,' said Troy, laughing, 'what
if everyone thought the way you do?
We wouldn't ever get rid of anything.
Those old freighters this afternoon,
for instance – would you have us keep
*them*?'

'Well, blowing them up doesn't

strike me as clever – just a big waste,' retorted Atlanta. 'I'm sure *somebody* could have found a use for them.'

Just then the videophone rang. It was Lieutenant Fischer, on duty at Marineville Tower. 'Yes, lieutenant?' said Commander Shore.

'Sorry to disturb you, sir,' said Fischer, 'but I was watching those old freighters on the radar, and. . . well . . .'

'Come on, man!' thundered Shore. 'And *what*?'

'Well, sir, I don't know how to explain it, but – they've disappeared!'

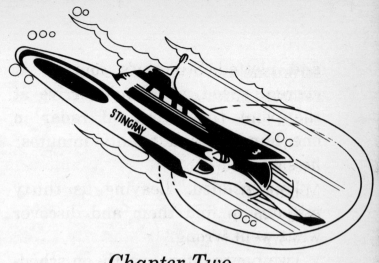

## Chapter Two
## SUNKEN HULKS

Commander Shore ordered Stingray
to put to sea at once. It was only
a matter of minutes before Troy,
Phones and Marina were speeding
towards the spot where the missing
freighters had disappeared.

'The first of the freighters is due to
detonate in two and a half hours,' said
Troy.

Phones checked the instruments

and plotted Stingray's course. 'At current speed, we should arrive at the point they went off radar in one hundred and twenty minutes,' he said.

Troy nodded. 'Leaving us thirty minutes to find them and discover what went wrong.'

Two hours later, exactly on schedule, they reached the area where the

ships had vanished. Troy tilted the beams of Stingray's powerful search-lights towards the sea bed and re-duced speed. They cruised low over the sand, the sudden light startling goggle-eyed fish that were more used to the continual green twilight of the ocean depths.

'No sign of the freighters,' muttered Troy. 'And yet, if they disappeared off the radar at this point, then they *must* have sunk.'

'Sure, skipper,' Phones agreed. 'But where are they?'

Marina nudged Troy's shoulder and pointed. He peered out through the viewport, then turned Stingray so that the searchlights stabbed off into the darkness where she was pointing. Sure enough, there was something there. With eyesight better suited to the murk of the ocean, Marina had spotted it before the two experienced aquanauts.

Stingray moved closer, and the beams picked out three deep furrows in the sand. The furrows led off beyond a ridge of sharp coral-covered rocks.

'It looks like something's been dragged along the sea bed,' was Phones's opinion.

'Something heavy,' said Troy. 'And three of them – it has to be the freighters. Let's follow the trail . . .'

Gliding over the sand like a great metal shark, Stingray tracked the furrows as they wound through swaying patches of seaweed and behind tall outcroppings of rock. At last, cresting a rise, they saw where the furrows led.

Troy and Phones gasped in awe.

They had seen many amazing sights in the course of their missions aboard Stingray, but nothing to compare to what lay ahead of them now.

'Shipwrecks . . .' said Phones. 'A whole *city* of shipwrecks . . .'

Dozens of ships were clustered around on the sea bed. Some looked more than a century old. And from every single one of the wrecks shone lights, making them look like huge buildings at night. Phones was right: it was an undersea city.

Marina pressed against the glass of the viewport. The people who lived aboard those wrecks might be her own kind. Before she had been enslaved by the evil Titan, she had lived a carefree roving life through the seas. Sometimes she too had used an old shipwreck for shelter. But she had never seen so many

all dragged together for the purpose. She wanted to swim out right away and find the people who lived there.

Troy glanced at her and guessed what she was thinking.

'Sorry, Marina,' he said, 'but we have to find the freighters first. Afterwards we can come back and investigate these old hulks.'

Stingray moved rapidly between the broken masts of the old ships. Marina stared out, straining for any sign of movement from the shipwreck dwellers. She thought she caught sight of faces peering up from the portholes of the nearest wreck, but they went past too fast for her to be certain.

The three furrows went right past the wrecks. Stingray followed them for another few hundred metres, then

Troy saw something that caused him to reduce speed.

'Look,' he said. 'The missing freighters.'

Troy cut the motors and Stingray drifted gently down to settle on the sea bed. As automatic motors moved back the steering columns, Troy and Phones leapt up and started to don their scuba suits.

Troy put through a radio call to Marineville. 'We've located the freighters,' he reported. 'Phones and I are going to swim over and take a look.'

'Fine, captain, but make it snappy,' replied Commander Shore. 'The first of those wrecks is set to blow in less than twenty minutes. You have to have Stingray well clear of the area by then.'

'Understood, sir,' answered Troy.

He turned off the radio. 'Marina, you stay here. And keep the hatch locked – the beings inhabiting that city of hulks might have seen Stingray go overhead, and we don't know if they're friendly or not. Come on, Phones.'

Troy and Phones left Stingray by means of the airlock in the prow. Marina could only watch from the cabin and wave. She hated being left behind when her friends were going into possible danger, but she knew they had specialized aquanaut training to help them react fast in emergencies. For all that she could breathe underwater, Marina was just a civilian. Of course it was useful to have somebody stay on board and keep an eye on Stingray, but that didn't make Marina feel any better. At times like this, she felt so useless.

Outside, Troy and Phones spoke

to each other over the short-range radios built into their oxygen masks. 'It's eerie, isn't it, skipper?' said Phones. 'Swimming up to a huge ship like this, I mean, when only a few hours ago we were standing on her deck.'

Troy had to agree. He had swum through wrecks before, of course, but it was always difficult to get used to the feeling. It was almost like some kind of a dream. Troy had sometimes had a dream like that, in which he came back home to find his whole apartment flooded underwater, and had to swim from room to room.

They swum over to the bridge of the nearest freighter. 'Keep your eyes peeled, Phones,' cautioned Troy. 'We don't yet know what we're dealing with.'

Fish flitted in and out of the

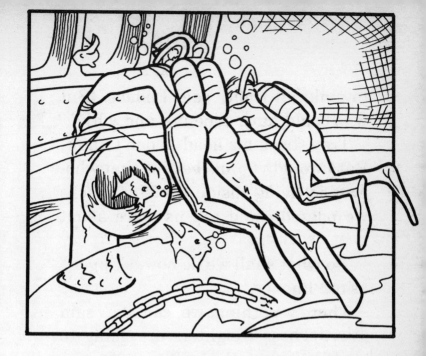

portholes as the two aquanauts approached. Other than that, the wreck was utterly deserted. Troy and Phones looked around the bridge for a clue as to why the freighter had sunk, but it was several minutes before they noticed that the sluice valves had been tampered with.

'Look at this, Phones,' said Troy. 'The valves have been opened.'

'That would have caused the ship

to sink, all right,' said Phones. 'But who could have done it – and why?'

Troy shook his head. 'I don't know. But I wouldn't mind betting that whoever is living inside the shipwrecks we passed could tell us more about it.'

'So what shall we do now, skipper?' asked Phones.

There's nothing we can do,' said Troy. 'These freighters are going to explode in less than fifteen minutes. We'd better go back to Stingray and get well clear of the blast zone. We can investigate the shipwreck city later.'

They swam back out of the freighter and started back towards Stingray. But they had not gone very far before something happened to change all their plans. A beam of sparkling ruby light lanced through the water, making a hissing sound as it went.

It narrowly missed Troy and Phones, and instead struck a boulder lying on the sea bed just in front of them. The boulder glowed red-hot, then was blasted apart into molten fragments.

'A laser gun!' shouted Troy. 'Someone's sniping at us!'

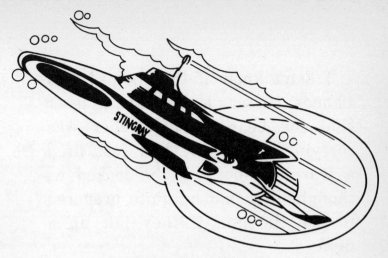

## Chapter Three
## RUSSIAN ROULETTE

Treading water, Troy and Phones looked around to see who had fired the shot. A figure emerged from behind some rocks. He wore long flowing robes, and his beard and long hair made him look like a Biblical prophet. Except that his skin was green.

'He's not of Marina's race,' observed Troy; 'but then again, at least he's not an aquaphibian . . .'

'I don't know if that helps,' said Phones. He was looking at the laser rifle the bearded sea-dweller was carrying. So far he had just fired a warning shot, but he looked as though he would be quite prepared to use the gun if they put up a fight.

Troy was thinking the same thing. As the sea-dweller pointed towards the sunken freighters, he said, 'He's got the drop on us. Don't make any sudden moves, Phones.'

The sea-dweller pointed at the aquanauts, then back at the nearest of the three freighters. After a moment, he emphasized what he was trying to tell them with a wave of his rifle muzzle.

'I think he wants us to go back aboard, skipper,' murmured Phones.

'Yeah,' said Troy, warily eyeing the

sea-dweller's rifle. 'Let's not keep him waiting.'

They followed the sea-dweller, who swam as nimbly as a fish despite his long robes and rather portly shape. Every so often he glanced back to make sure they didn't try to get away. As the three of them drew near to the freighter, the sea-sweller led them towards the lower part of the stern.

'That's funny,' Troy remarked. 'He's not heading for the bridge.'

Reaching the hull, the sea-dweller touched a button and a metal door slid open. He turned to level the rifle at the aquanauts as they swam up.

'Wow!' said Phones, looking through the open doorway. 'It's a makeshift airlock. This guy and his pals sure work fast!'

Troy was still watching the sea-dweller. If they had been on dry land,

he was now close enough to make a grab for the rifle. But Troy knew that would be suicide here, underwater. He couldn't hope to move fast enough to get the rifle away before the sea-dweller pulled the trigger.

The sea-dweller may have guessed what was going through the W.A.S.P. captain's mind. He hefted the gun purposefully and nodded towards the airlock.

Reluctantly, Troy and Phones entered, followed by their captor. The door slid shut behind them and there was a bubbling as air replaced the water around them. After a minute, the airlock had drained. A door opened in the far wall and they stepped through into the interior of the freighter.

Troy pulled off his scuba mask. 'Look here,' he demanded of the sea-dweller, 'just what are you playing at?'

The sea-dweller smiled and waved them over to a couch, but he kept the rifle trained on them the whole time. 'My name is Pagurus,' he told them. 'My people are a race of hermit no-mads who have lived here under the ocean for centuries.'

'How come you breathe air?' asked Phones.

'Like dolphins, we have no gills,' said Pagurus. 'We are not fish! But I shall ask the questions, terraneans: why did you come here?'

'We needed to find out what made these freighters sink,' explained Troy. 'I guess we've got our answer, now.'

'You had abandoned these vessels,' said Pagurus defensively; 'you had no further use for them. My people, on the other hand, can put them to good use. We need new homes to replace our old ones, which are rotten with age.'

'Your *homes*?' said Phones. 'You mean that cluster of old wrecks we passed over? That's where you live?'

Pagurus nodded. 'But they are very old. Most of them leak, and it is time for us to find new vessels.'

Phones sighed. 'Well, you sure picked the wrong ones this time, pal.'

'That's right,' put in Troy. 'These ships are scheduled for demolition. If you could read our language, you'd know that's what the letters on the side of the hull stood for. The first ship is due to blow up in just a few minutes . . .'

Pagurus glared at him. His bushy beard and huge eyebrows made him look very fierce as he snarled, 'You're lying! You terraneans always lie! If these ships were going to explode, you would hardly have risked your own lives by coming here.'

'It's our duty,' Troy explained. 'We had to find out why the ships sank. Now believe me, the first of the ships is set to explode in less than five minutes from now – and, for all I know, it could be this one!'

Troy had spoken vehemently, but amazingly Pagurus' only answer was a placid smile. He still thought they were lying!

'Come on, Phones,' snapped Troy. 'We have to get out of here.'

Pagurus' smile vanished. He raised the laser rifle and pointed it straight at them. 'You will stay where you are,' he said commandingly. 'When my fellow nomads return from their foraging expedition, the whole tribe will decide what is to be done with you.'

'By that time all three of us will be no good for anything but fish bait!' said Troy. He glanced at his watch. 'Barely four minutes now . . .'

The minutes sped by. Beads of sweat formed on the faces of the two aquanauts as they waited helplessly, not even knowing if the ship they were on would be the first to explode.

'Just a matter of seconds now, skipper,' muttered Phones.

Troy nodded, weighing up the odds. Whichever way he looked at it, their chances were not good. The main explosive charges were packed towards the centre of each freighter, whereas the compartment they were sitting in was at the stern – but even if they didn't die in the blast, the shockwave was sure to get them. When the hull split, it would be like being hit by a ton of falling rubble.

Troy crossed his fingers. There was nothing else he could do. The last seconds slid away . . .

A blast thundered against the hull, rocking the huge freighter and sending them flying across the small cabin. There was a metallic rattling from outside as fragments of debris from one of the other freighters shot out from the blast.

'Hear that?' Troy snapped at Pagurus. 'That was the first freighter blowing up. We're lucky it wasn't this one, or we'd all be dead now!'

Pagurus rubbed his head, dazed. Not having been braced for the shockwave, he had fallen heavily against the bulkhead, his laser rifle crashing to the ground beside him. 'I . . . believe you, now, terranean . . .' he

gasped. 'We must get out of here . . .'

'We can't,' said Phones suddenly. 'Look at the door to the airlock.'

They stared in horror at the sight. The powerful shockwave had driven debris against the hull, buckling the door-frame so that the door was jammed.

'It won't budge!' said Troy, after straining with all his strength to force the door open. 'We're trapped in here.'

'There's only ten minutes before the next blast,' said Phones. 'And it's an even bet that it'll be *this* ship next time. It's like playing Russian Roulette . . .'

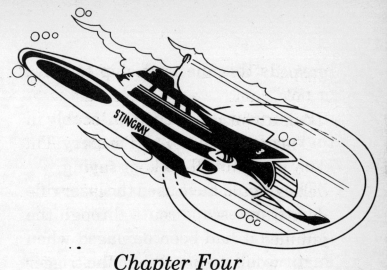

## *Chapter Four*
## BLIND LUCK

'This is madness!' cried Troy in frustration. 'Just waiting to die . . .!'

They struggled in vain to turn the wheel that opened the door but it was badly buckled from the explosion and the door was stuck fast. Now they could only sit and wait as the minutes passed.

'We'll soon know,' said Phones, wiping the cold film of sweat off his brow. 'Is this the next ship to blow, or not?'

Pagurus was hunched miserably in the corner of the cabin. 'I'm sorry, I'm sorry . . .' was all he kept saying.

They would have used the laser rifle to blast an escape route through the hull, but it had been damaged when Pagurus fell earlier. When the trigger was pressed it just emitted a stuttering hum and a pencil-thin beam of dim light. Some vital element had obviously been broken beyond repair.

Exasperated, Troy hammered at the airlock door with the butt of the broken rifle. 'We can't give up!' he said. 'Not while we still have breath in our lungs.'

Phones looked at his watch. 'It's now,' he said.

There was the roar of a titanic

explosion from outside the hull. Waves of water slammed into their own ship with crushing force. The ship swayed under the impact, and the three of them were sent hurtling against the cabin walls.

Stunned by the force of the blast, it was several minutes before any of them stirred.

Troy was the first to recover consciousness. *That's odd*, he thought, tasting salt water on his lips. Suddenly he came fully awake and jumped up, ignoring the pain where he had bumped his head. 'Phones!' he yelled. 'Water's getting in somewhere!'

Phones gave a groan and sat up, nursing his head. 'But I don't understand, skipper,' he replied. 'How can it be?'

Troy looked around to see where the water was coming in. 'It's the air-lock door,' he said.

Around the edge of the door, water was indeed now trickling in. 'The second blast must have loosened it,' said Phones. He tried turning the wheel that winched the door open. It shifted a short distance and then stuck again. There was now a gap between the door and the frame; it was about as wide as a man's fist. Water came sluicing in faster now.

Troy lifted his watch. The face was cracked; he must have hit it against something when he fell. 'How long have we got, Phones?' he asked.

'Just five minutes, Troy,' said Phones, checking his own watch.

'Fetch that broken rifle,' Troy ordered. 'We can use it as a lever. Maybe with all three of us trying

together, we can force the door open.'

Pausing only to replace their scuba masks, they set to work. With muscles straining, they forced the door open inch by agonizing inch. The water was now gushing in and it was difficult to keep one's balance, but the dauntless aquanauts struggled on.

Finally their efforts were rewarded by a grinding of metal as the door gradually eased open.

'Is there room for us to squeeze through?' wondered Phones, looking at the gap.

'Time's running out,' said Troy. 'It's now or never.'

Scrambling through the broken air-lock, they emerged from the freighter with only thirty seconds to spare. They could see Marina inside Sting-ray's cabin, waving her arms excitedly as she watched them swimming

closer. She had waited all this time, torn by anguish as she witnessed the destruction of the first two vessels. She might have switched Stingray to automatic control at any time, to carry herself safely clear of the blast zone, but she had refused to abandon her comrades.

Troy, Phones and Pagurus swam into Stingray's open hatch and rushed up the companion-way to the cabin. Phones looked at his watch. 'Ten seconds, Troy,' he said.

Troy glanced over towards the third freighter. They were much too close. Stingray would be caught up in the explosion if they stayed here. He jabbed at the emergency booster and there was a ripple of unleashed energy through Stingray's hull as the atomic hydrojets fired up.

Stingray soared up from the sea

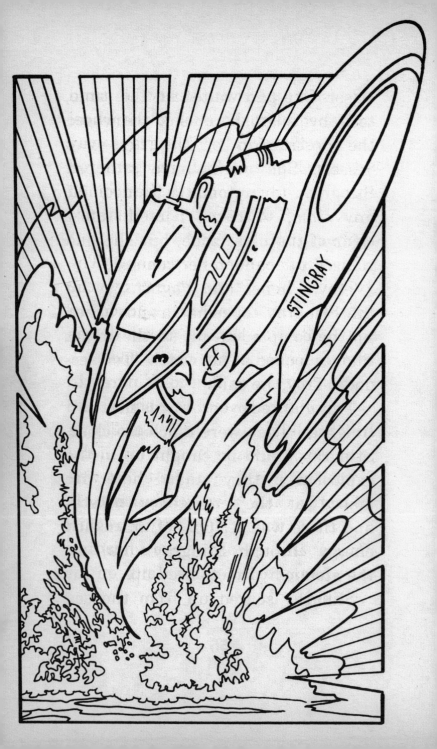

bed, stirring up a flurry of sand and weeds. Troy wrenched the wheel to one side, turning Stingray away from the blast zone. As they gathered speed, the others watched the doomed freighter recede into the distance behind them.

The last seconds ran out. The freighter was torn apart by the tons of high explosive packed in her hold. Chunks of metal debris were flung across the ocean floor.

The shockwave caused Stingray to judder in her course. She shook like an aeroplane in a storm, but Troy's prompt action had got them out of the danger zone in time. The effect was no worse than heavy turbulence. It took only moments for Troy to regain control, and then they were heading back towards the nomad city on an even keel.

'Darn,' said Troy, looking at the smashed dial of his watch. 'This was a present from Atlanta.'

Phones settled into his chair and breathed a huge sigh of relief. 'Skipper,' he said, 'I'll buy you a *dozen* new watches if you like, once we get home to Marineville.'

A couple of weeks later, Troy and Phones met at Commander Shore's apartment for their regular card game.

'We got rid of another three obsolete ships yesterday,' said the commander. 'How many is that in all?'

Troy counted them up in his head. 'Must be . . . oh, twenty ships over the last fortnight.'

Phones nodded. 'It's a neat arrangement,' he said. 'We just send them to the bottom, and Pagurus and his hermit nomads convert them into homes.'

Commander Shore grunted as he rummaged through a drawer full of junk, looking for a fresh pack of cards. 'You see what you've done, Troy?' he grumbled good-naturedly. 'By making me agree to let that undersea race have our old ships, you've lost me my argument with Atlanta. This place is going to be packed with any old rubbish from now on!'

Atlanta came in a put a pack of cards on the table. 'I think this is what you're looking for, father,' she said with a grin.

'Great,' said Phones. 'Now maybe we can get on with the game.'

Troy shook his head. 'Count me out,' he said. 'I'm giving up gambling from now on. I just don't think I'm the lucky type!'

Commander Shore sighed and tore up the piece of paper on which he tallied their scores. 'In that case I may as well forget about the seven million, three hundred thousand and eighty dollars you owe me,' he said. 'Still . . . on your salary it would've taken you over a hundred years to pay it off, anyhow.'

Phones shuffled the cards and dealt hands to himself and the others.

The commander fanned his cards and studied them intently for a few moments. Then his weather-beaten face broke into a triumphant smile. 'OK, Phones, I'll raise you one million dollars.'

*'One million dollars!'* Phones wailed.

'Yeah, one million dollars!' barked Commander Shore. 'What's the matter with you, man? Can't you stand a little *risk* now and again?'

**THE END**

## STINGRAY TITLES AVAILABLE FROM YOUNG CORGI

THE PRICES SHOWN BELOW WERE CORRECT AT THE TIME
OF GOING TO PRESS. HOWEVER TRANSWORLD PUBLISHERS
RESERVE THE RIGHT TO SHOW NEW RETAIL PRICES ON COVERS
WHICH MAY DIFFER FROM THOSE PREVIOUSLY ADVERTISED IN
THE TEXT OR ELSEWHERE.

❏ 0 552 527785  **STINGRAY: TRAPPED IN THE DEPTHS**
*Dave Morris* £2.50
❏ 0 552 527793  **STINGRAY: MARINEVILLE TRAITOR**
*Dave Morris* £2.50
❏ 0 552 527807  **STINGRAY: THE DISAPPEARING SHIPS**
*Dave Morris* £2.50
❏ 0 552 527815  **STINGRAY: THE LIGHTHOUSE DWELLERS**
*Dave Morris* £2.50

All Young Corgi Books are available at your bookshop or newsagent,
or can be ordered from the following address:

Transworld Publishers
Cash Sales Department
P.O. Box 11, Falmouth, Cornwall TR10 9EN

Please send a cheque or postal order (no currency) and allow £1.00 for
postage and packing for one book, an additional 50p for a second book,
and an additional 30p for each subsequent book ordered to a maximum
charge of £3.00 if ordering seven or more books.

Overseas customers, including Eire, please allow £2.00 for postage and
packing for the first book, an additional £1.00 for a second book, and
an additional 50p for each subsequent title ordered.

NAME (Block letters) .........................................................................................

ADDRESS.........................................................................................

.........................................................................................